Praise for Odette's Alphabet

"Inspiring and practical, *Odette's Alphabet* offers a beautiful invitation to embrace who we truly are—it's a gift for children and parents."

—Marci Shimoff, *New York Times* bestselling author,
Happy for No Reason and *Chicken Soup for the Woman's Soul*

"*Odette's Alphabet* is the perfect guide to teach kids the power of creating an internal sacred space. It is a charming, compelling, and heartwarming story about friendship, adventure, happiness, and peace. It is the perfect gift for children and parents!"

—Terri Cole, psychotherapist, author of *Boundary Boss*

"*Odette's Alphabet* is a playful introduction to mindfulness that can be helpful to children and adults alike. My analytical son, who is not easily impressed, gave it the highest praise when he said, 'This book is awesome. I wish I had this book when I was a kid.'"

—John Paul Abner, PhD, parent child interaction therapy
international master trainer, professor of psychology, Milligan University;
John-Phillip Abner, film student, Syracuse University

"*Odette's Alphabet* will warm your bookshelf with light and love. I can't wait to share the story and meditation activities with my young son. It's more than a story—it's a handbook on how to look within and find refuge, joy, and peace."

—Kate Doyle, human resources officer, United Nations

"This book is a sweet gem for children! I can't wait to explore it with my seven-year-old twins and my toddler."

—Ellen D. Buckley, social studies teacher,
Midwood High School, Brooklyn

"Explore the beauty and simplicity of meditation through Odette and Marcus's beautiful journey, which speaks to anyone at any age. This book is wonderful and filled with love and light. The world needs this."

—Valerie Oula, author of *A Little Bit of Reiki* and *Rest Rituals*,
vibrational energy director at The Well

More praise for *Odette's Alphabet*

"With vivid storytelling and endearing illustrations, *Odette's Alphabet* introduces both mindfulness concepts and practice to young children. The beauty of this combination is that children learn how mindful moments can be captured throughout their day—integrated in their actions—and how that doesn't need to look like the mindfulness practice they (may) see adults engage in. This book, being an early entrée to becoming attuned to one's own thoughts and feelings, is a welcome addition to any child's bookcase or library."

—Karina Mackenzie, VP of programming, Wanderlust

"When it comes to children's books, there are loads of options, millions to choose from, but the mindfulness, kindness, and tools Sandrine shares in this book are a gift to children. Imagine if we all had the awareness that we do now, the tools to help manage our emotions, mind, and stress. It's woven in such a clever way throughout *Odette's Alphabet* for children to comprehend and parents to share with their little ones. We can all learn from *Odette's Alphabet*, no matter our age . . . the messages have no limit. The world would be a calmer place if we all practiced them a little more often. I look forward to a future series, children need more of this!"

—Sara Wright, business strategist and connector

"I love *Odette's Alphabet* and think it is the perfect activity for me and my boys to share together each day. We all feel stressed (adults and children), and this is a fun way to help find our peace and presence to start our day. Sweet, simple, and easy for any age to understand, *Odette's Alphabet* is a great reminder to stop and be more present."

—Amanda Judge, mother of two,
owner and designer of UntamedPetals

"This book is absolutely beautiful! I cried—the message is so beautiful and really tender."

—Emily Metzger, photographer

Odette's Alphabet

written by **Sandrine Marlier**

illustrations by **Leonardo Schiavina**

BELLE ISLE BOOKS
www.belleislebooks.com

ISBN: 978-1-953021-51-9
LCCN: 2022915355

Project managed by Grace Ball

Printed in the United States of America

Published by
Belle Isle Books (an imprint of Brandylane Publishers, Inc.)
5 S. 1st Street
Richmond, Virginia 23219

BELLE ISLE BOOKS
www.belleislebooks.com

belleislebooks.com | brandylanepublishers.com

*To Emma, my greatest teacher
and the sparkled rainbow of my life.*

Foreword

Resting deep inside each one of us is a peaceful, calm, and happy place. We feel it when we give a hug, spend time in nature, play with our friends, laugh, and lay in bed at night before we fall asleep. But every morning when we wake up, we never know what the next moment will bring—a celebration or a challenge, an excitement or a fear, a disappointment or a happiness.

We can't control the world around us, but we always have the ability to bring ourselves back to that safe place inside of us . . . the place of the present moment . . . of calm . . . and of joy.

Using the alphabet, the magical ant Odette and her new pal, Marcus, take us on a beautiful journey of discovery, one where we can find our way back home to peace, happiness, and the sweet, safe, special space that rests inside—through spending time in nature, meeting new friends, celebrating our differences, listening to our hearts, thinking good thoughts, and connecting to our breath.

It is a magnificent journey, and in the process, we'll learn to meditate and live our lives from the inside out! Have fun!!!

—davidji, author of *Secrets of Meditation*

Odette wakes up one day feeling out of sorts. She can hear the colony already busy at work. As she gets ready for the day, she just can't shake the feeling that something is wrong. Odette's not as calm as she usually is. She can feel her heart beating really fast.

Odette has been working in the colony for a long time. She loves the other ants, but they all work too much! There is just not enough time to relax.

When Odette picks up her bag, she feels her heart beating even faster than it was before. Then, Odette understands what's happening—she's feeling stressed!

She drops her bag to the floor and steps out of her room.

A

Alive

Odette slides down the long exit tunnel that's just outside her room and lands on soft ground. She looks up and smiles. Spangles of light move all around her, and she already feels better.

Odette jumps up in the air and feels so alive! It's as if the sunlight is moving inside her.

Activity: Stand up and feel your feet touching the ground. Take three long, slow, deep breaths, in through your nose and out through your mouth. Imagine sparkles of light tickling the soles of your feet, swimming up to your belly, and reaching your hands and face. Now, sweep your arms up over your head and say out loud or to yourself: "I am alive!" You may want to jump up in the air and say it one more time.

Do this any time you feel a little down, and it will cheer you up.

B Breath

Odette takes the deepest breath of her life, in and out. And again, in and—

"Achoo!"—Odette looks around to find where the noise came from, and she sees a mouse hiding under a large flower. The mouse comes out slowly, shivering and sniffling.

"Hi, I'm Marcus," the mouse says. "I'm lost, and . . . I'm scared."

Remembering how good it felt to just breathe, Odette invites Marcus to take a deep breath in and out with her.

Activity: *Place your hands on your belly. Take a deep breath in. Feel your belly grow big and round like a balloon. Slowly exhale to release the balloon, relaxing your neck, shoulders, and belly. Can you give the balloon a color? How does that color make you feel? Repeat this process until you feel completely relaxed.*

C Community

As Odette and Marcus take deep breaths in and out, Odette thinks about her colony and how everyone is able to work together so well—all the ants help each other. And because of this, they accomplish amazing things, like building nests in trees! To succeed, the ants have to work together, but they also have to develop their own special skills and different talents. Odette loves being part of a community and knowing there's a place where she belongs, where she matters to everyone. She wants Marcus to have that too.

Between deep breaths, Odette says to Marcus, "I'll help you find your way home."

Activity: Place one hand on your chest and feel it rising as you inhale and relaxing as you exhale. With your fingertips, start tapping your chest and collarbone gently. Continue tapping and say out loud: "I am safe. I am important. I am enough." Do this three times. Then, place your arms around your body and give yourself a nice big hug. Is there someone you'd like to give a hug to?

D Different

Marcus looks at Odette, unsure if he can trust her. She has six legs and two antennae. Marcus wonders where her tail is, and why her ears don't look the same as his. Odette and Marcus look so different!

Odette reaches out and places her hand on his. The gentle pressure reminds Marcus of the way his big sister places her hand on his back to reassure him when he's scared. Marcus smiles. Maybe Odette is not so different from him after all. . . .

Activity: Find a partner and look into each other's eyes. You may want to hold hands. If your eyes could hear your partner's eyes, what would they tell you about your partner? If your eyes could talk to your partner's, what would they say? Notice how it feels to communicate with the eyes alone.

It's easy to forget, but together, let's remember that beyond appearances and differences, there are only shared and common experiences.

E   Explore

Odette looks beyond Marcus, over to the flower he was hiding under, and spots a path. She points to it and asks, "Marcus, did you use that path to get here?"

"I'm not sure. It looks familiar," Marcus says. "But I can't be certain that path will lead to my home."

"There's only way to find out," Odette says.

Marcus is a little nervous. He takes a deep breath in and out. Still holding hands, Odette and Marcus step onto the path stretching before them.

Activity: Sit in a comfortable position and either place your fingers in your ears or cup your ears with your hands. You should hear your breath hiss gently like the ocean. Continue breathing this way for several rounds. Imagine your belly is an ocean and your breath is the current. The inhales and the exhales are the waves—soft and gentle. Perhaps you see yourself surfing on those waves.

What differences do you notice when you breathe from your ocean belly?

F

Flower

Marcus can't help but notice all the lovely flowers as he and Odette walk along the path. Fluffy fuchsias stand tall and arch over them. Marcus pauses to breathe in the fragrance and smiles.

"The scent of the flowers makes me feel so alive!" he says.

Odette laughs and gives him a high five.

Activity: *Find a scent you like in a lotion or an oil. (Make sure it is safe to use on your skin.) Rub it between your palms, close your eyes, and take a long, slow, deep breath in. Pause. Feel the scent entering your nostrils, head, and body, and slowly release it. Do this two more times, breathing in the scent of calm and slowly exhaling, relaxing, and softening your heart and belly.*

Can you go to a park or garden today and greet the flowers you find in the same way? Flowers are like colorful teachers. They make you stop to breathe a little deeper and help you feel a little calmer.

G

Grow

As Marcus explores with Odette, his joy and confidence grow. The two are walking along the path when, out of nowhere, a big bubble appears, and Marcus feels so brave, he steps inside!

Odette bursts out laughing and notices her own heart grows too. She's feeling better and better.

Activity: Sit comfortably. Relax your shoulders, arms, and face. Take a few deep breaths through the nose, nice and even. Close your eyes and start imagining a bubble inside your chest. You may color it any way you like; this is your bubble. With each new breath you take, the bubble slowly grows. Soon, it grows so big that you find yourself inside of it.

Know that you are safe, surrounded with peace and love. Stay here for as long as you like.

H

Home

After walking for a while, the path begins to look more and more familiar to Marcus. Soon, he comes to a stop and points to a nearby house. "Home!" he says.

Odette is happy that her new friend has found his way home, but she's also sad to say goodbye. She thinks about going back to her own home, and her heart starts beating fast again.

Just then, Marcus exclaims, "I have an idea!" and dashes into his house. He returns with paper and a pen. "Let's draw a map of where I live. That way, I'll never get lost again!"

Odette helps Marcus draw a map of his house and all the paths they came across on their way. Marcus looks excitedly at the map, but Odette still can't help but feel nervous about her own return home.

Activity: In the middle of a large piece of paper, draw all the people, animals, activities, and things that are important to you. Take your time to draw in what sparks joy for you. Then, draw a house around it all. Guess what you've drawn? A place that feels like home!

I Imagine

"Now that I know how to go home," Marcus says, "let's go explore and have some fun!" He pulls on Odette's hand and says, "Let's go on a brand-new adventure!"

Odette didn't know she would have such a day when she woke up this morning. But the more she imagines what her day could feel like, the more it becomes that way.

"I imagine a world where we can live and work in peace and love, all the time," Odette says.

Now it's Marcus's turn to laugh and give Odette a big high five.

Activity: Get comfortable. Take three slow, deep breaths and close your eyes. Imagine your perfect day, a day where you feel calm, happy, and at ease. Feel all the sensations in your body. What do you most wish would happen today? Picture it happening. Imagine anything you want; your imagination knows no limit!

Know that you can come back to this picture in your head throughout the day, to this special place in your imagination, anytime you wish and as often as you like.

J

Joy

Odette is having so much fun with Marcus today! She can't remember the last time she played and laughed like this. Her time outside the colony feels so special. She can fully be herself here. There's no stress. Just joy. There's nothing to do but simply be. She imagines what it would be like to feel that way every day. . . .

Activity: Think of a moment that sparked a lot of joy for you. Who was there? What was happening? What were you doing? Now, make a list of three specific things that always bring you joy. Pick one for today and go do it! Tonight, at dinnertime, how would it feel to share your experience?

K   Kindness

With Marcus's map in hand, Odette and Marcus leave his house behind for more nature. They follow the sun and the scent of their favorite flowers. As they walk along the open road, they find a broken tree. To Odette, the trunk looks like an ant colony. Odette is reminded of her home, and she starts feeling really stressed again. All the joy she felt before floats away.

Marcus gets another idea. He picks up a fluffy fuchsia flower from the side of the road and offers it to Odette.

"Marcus, you're so kind!" she says, and a smile returns to her face.

Activity: Start by breathing in on the count of four, hold your breath for two, and breathe out for four. Do this three times. Now think of some kind things people have done for you recently. How did that make you feel? Can you think of one kind thing you could do for someone today? How would it feel to do that?

L

Love

As Marcus and Odette follow the path, Odette thinks about how, in the colony, ants can sometimes be too busy to show their love for each other, but Odette feels a lot of love for all the other ants. She puts a hand on her heart and imagines the ants right beside her. Her heart grows so big it feels like it will explode if she doesn't share some of that love! So, she sends love to all her friends, like the sun sends rays of sunshine to the Earth. She sends love to everyone, like the clouds send rain to the fields. Like magic, it all comes back to her—times a million! Love is funny that way: the more we give, the more we receive.

Activity: Get comfortable. Take a few deep breaths, nice and slow, and close your eyes. Think of all those you love and imagine they are right inside your heart, even if they are very far away. Imagine sparkles of light tickling your heart. Feel this light grow big like a balloon. This balloon is now so big your heart is bursting with love for all those dear to you and even for those you don't know. Breathe in this love you feel and breathe out this love to everyone.

M   Meditation

Odette and Marcus keep walking until they come to a fork in the road, where a large fig tree stands. They look right and they look left, but they don't know which way to go.

Odette sits down with her back against the trunk of the tree. Marcus joins her, and together, they take some deep breaths in and deep breaths out. They feel the ground underneath their feet and let their bodies relax. They close their eyes and imagine that the right path lies before them.

"I feel so calm," Odette says. "It's as if the roots of this tree are supporting me."

"I feel at home under this tree," Marcus says in turn. "And I feel strong!"

Activity: Sit someplace comfortable, with your feet touching the ground. Take three deep breaths and relax every part of your body, slowly, one at a time. Imagine the soles of your feet connecting with the roots of a tree, feeling safe and supported by the earth. Watch your breath, flowing in and out of your nostrils. Whenever a thought arises, name it in silence: "thought," and let it pass by you like a cloud in the sky. Gently come back to your breath. Keep going for the next few minutes.

N Nature

When Odette and Marcus open their eyes, they both feel so open and relaxed! They look at the fluffy flowers and the fig tree, and they see that the nature around them also seems open and relaxed.

"I am like this tree," Odette says.

"And I am like these flowers," Marcus chimes in.

They all seem to be breathing and relaxing together.

"In nature, we are all one and the same!" Odette exclaims.

Activity: Sit comfortably, rest your hands on your lap, and close your eyes. Visualize your spine, from your tailbone to the top of your head. Take a few deep breaths, keeping them slow and even. Imagine you are sitting by a tree, and golden leaves are around you on the ground. As you breathe in, picture the golden leaves flying up along your spine. As you exhale, the leaves gently fall down along your spine, back to the ground. You are feeling more and more relaxed.

O   Optimism

Odette stands up and walks around the large tree. She notices a sign she had not seen before. It points in one direction and reads "Optimism."

"What does that mean?" Marcus asks.

"It means we have to think positive thoughts to get to the place we want to be," Odette explains.

"Okay," Marcus says. "Let's follow the sign!"

Activity: When you wake up, plant your feet on the ground and tell yourself this magical phrase: "Something amazing is going to happen today; let's find out what it is!" How do you feel after you've said that? Would you like to try doing this every morning for a week? If you want to become an expert at being an optimist, expect the best in life!

P

Peace

As Odette walks the path of optimism, she imagines what it would feel like if there was more time for laughing, sharing, and relaxing in the colony. It would be so peaceful! She knows there is another way to live and work, but how can she help change their way of doing things?

Activity: Let's play "I am peace" using our fingers. Say "I" while touching your thumb to your index finger, say "am" while touching your thumb to your middle finger, and say "peace" while touching your thumb to your ring finger. "I. Am. Peace." Say it three times, very slowly. Then whisper it three times. And now, repeat it in silence, in your mind.

Did this help you feel a little more at peace?

Q

Quiet

Odette thinks of the constant hustle and bustle in the tunnels and chambers of the colony. There are always eggs and baby ants to take care of, food to gather for everyone, and lots of building work. It never stops!

Outside the colony, life is much quieter. All Odette can hear now are the birds chirping. How can she find peace and quiet amongst all the noise back home?

Activity: Find a quiet spot and get settled. Place your hands in front of your face and breathe into them. Feel the warmth of your breath in your hands as you exhale and feel the coolness of your breath as you inhale. Do three rounds. Now, listen to the silence in the room. Take your time. Notice how this feels. Then, pay attention to any sounds you can hear. Notice how this feels. Can you still feel peace and quiet inside?

R

Relax

Odette stops walking.

"What's going on?" Marcus asks.

"I'm feeling stressed again."

"Odette, take some deep breaths and let yourself relax."

Odette places her attention on her breath, watching it come in and out. Within just a few seconds, she feels peace and quiet inside. "It's so fast to relax," she says. "All we have to do is breathe!"

Activity: Put some relaxing music on and lie down on your back. Imagine that you are heavy like a tree, the sun shining bright over you. Let your body sink into the ground, melting with each breath you take. Your head, shoulders, arms, buttocks, and legs have never felt so heavy. So warm. You can let yourself completely relax knowing that you are safe and that the earth's got your back. Stay as long as you like, breathing and relaxing.

S

Smile

Odette feels happy. She's smiling so big that Marcus gets another idea—another great idea!

"When you go back to the colony, you could teach them how to meditate!"

Odette's eyes open wide. She loved meditating by the tree earlier. It felt calming and exciting. She also remembers how easily the solution to their problem appeared after meditating. Maybe the other ants would benefit from what she's learned today. . . .

Now the thought of going home makes Odette so happy she could smile for miles.

Activity: Get comfortable. Take a few slow and steady breaths and become present in your body. Close your eyes and picture a deep blue sky—a benevolent sky with a smile. You can trust that everything is and will be okay. You surrender to this moment. Soon, your face merges with the sky, your eyes smile gently, and your lips curl up. Rest in this smiley sky above you for a few minutes. When you go out today, remember the smile in the sky!

T Thank You

"Thank you, Marcus. You're such a good friend. I feel so much better." Odette has learned a lot from her friend and from their adventure together. Perhaps the most important lesson she's received is that peace begins within. If you want peace in the world, you must first feel peace in your heart.

Marcus is grateful for their new friendship too—he felt so lost and scared before he met Odette. He's learned to trust others, and he's also learned to trust himself.

"I think I'm ready to go home," Odette says.

Activity: Odette's attitude of gratitude gives her even greater joy. Before going to bed, it is fun to think of all the things that we are grateful for. Would you like to try? Or try starting a gratitude journal! Begin the day by writing three things that you are grateful for. Notice how it makes you feel afterward.

U Unique

Now that Odette has found her unique gift—spreading peace and joy through meditation—she looks like a beam of light, with sparkles everywhere. When Marcus met Odette, he was a little scared—they looked so different. But Odette is more than different: she's unique! You don't have to be especially good at something to be unique. The special fact that you are you makes you unique. There's no one else like you! When you see others as unique, it transforms the world like magic.

Activity: Do you know what your special gift is? Ask yourself what sparks joy in you. What is important to you? What makes you feel alive? If you're not sure, you can ask your friends and family, they will know. Once you've found out what your unique gift is, please share it! The world can only shine bright if it has that special light that only you carry. Can you think of a way you can help others using your special gift?

Remember, even if you don't know yet what your gift is, you are unique—just by being you.

V

Volunteer

Marcus, too, has a unique gift: he makes amazing maps!

"From now on," he says, "I will help anyone I come across who is lost find their way home." Marcus pulls out his map and adds a few more lines. "I'll make maps for everyone!"

Activity: Close your eyes and get ready for a journey into the sky. Imagine you can fly. Breathe in and start lifting. Breathe out and pass high above forests, rivers, and mountains. You feel so free and brave. Soon, you notice someone who is struggling below. You wish to help that person. You pause somewhere safe and wish for that person to find more ease. It's working! This brings you a sense of peace and joy. Gently and safely, you return to the place where you started, seated. Take time to come back to the room, feel your feet on the ground, and when you're ready, open your eyes.

Think of one way you could volunteer to help someone you know is having a hard time. Is there a place you could help feed the homeless, donate clothes, or even plant a tree? What can you do to help today, even just a little bit?

W

Wonder

When they awoke this morning, Odette and Marcus didn't know something as amazing as their new friendship was going to happen, but it did. Odette didn't know peace and joy were so easy to cultivate, but they are. Marcus didn't know the world could be such a wonderful place to grow and explore, but it is. Now, they know anything is possible!

When you look at the world with a sense of wonder, as if it were your first time seeing it, life is truly wonderful. Odette and Marcus have grown into two true optimists!

Activity: Get comfortable. Ask yourself how you are feeling to-day. Using gentle finger pressure, lightly tap the top of your head and repeat out loud three times: "Even though I sometimes feel [worried/ scared/ sad/ angry]," move to the point between your eyebrows and gently tap there, repeating three times: "I deeply love and accept myself." Tap around the eyes, under the eyes, under the nose, and on your chin. Beat your chest area and repeat: "I know everything will be okay." Tap under your arm like a monkey. Stop and rest for a minute. How was this experience for you?

X

XOXO

Odette sees that she and Marcus are getting closer to her colony. She looks toward the anthill she left this morning. She writes a note to Marcus on the back of his map, thanking him for his friendship and signing XOXO at the bottom.

"What does that mean?" Marcus asks.

"It means hugs and kisses." She pauses and asks, "Can I give you a hug, Marcus?" He agrees, and they both smile.

"I've got a gift for you too!' Marcus says, pulling out another piece of paper. "I drew you a separate map that shows the path from your home to mine!"

Odette and Marcus promise to meet again soon, and each feels their heart grow a little more.

Activity: *Get comfortable and place your attention on your breath, gently letting it flow in and out of you. Place your hands on your heart and follow the movements of your chest. Simply observe, eyes closed. Sit and wait for sensations to arise. Can you feel your heart beating? It may feel warm or vibrating with energy. Stay there, as if you could breathe through your chest. What would it be like to send this energy you feel in your heart to your entire body? Enjoy this energy coming from your heart and let it shine!*

Y

Yoga

The sunset light warms Odette's face. She's just outside the anthill, and Odette is a little nervous to go inside. She wishes there were a tree nearby she could sit under to meditate. As she relaxes using all the tricks and techniques she's discovered today, she gets an idea! She takes the shape of a tree to remember how wonderful it felt to sit under the tree. Her breath makes her feel one with the world, and Odette is grateful to have a place to call home.

Activity: Stand tall and find your center. Feel the ground underneath your feet and feel its roots supporting you. Now, balance on one foot, and place your other foot against your opposite leg. Pretend you are a tree! You may stretch your arms out as if they were branches. Can you feel yourself growing?

Z

Zen

Odette climbs up the long tunnel to the main chamber of the colony, and she's met with celebratory applause. All the ants are so happy to see her that they stop working, and Odette gives hugs and kisses. They all want to hear her story. Many ants have also been feeling stressed lately.

A few weeks later, Marcus comes to visit his friend. He sees Odette leading a meditation class, everyone inhaling, exhaling, and looking peaceful. The entire colony seems to be in a state of Zen—happy and relaxed.

Activity: Take a big breath in, fill up your lungs, and exhale gently, emptying your lungs. Do this three times. Take a new deep breath in and, on the exhale, release the sound "OM," first with slightly open mouth, then lips together, humming the sound "OM." Can you feel the vibration in your chest? Do this three times.

What have you learned from Odette's story? Can you share something you've learned? I bet you can teach a thing or two to someone else, just like Odette!

Acknowledgments

I am forever grateful to all the people who have helped shape *Odette's Alphabet*, a project I feel so passionate about.

To all my teachers, especially davidji, I say thank you. Odette started out as a doodle while I sat in a makeup chair observing an ant walking along a windowsill, and she came to life on the last day of my meditation teacher training, speaking her very first sound: "A"— and her universe was born.

Thank you to other mentors and teachers, such as Valerie Oula, Joanna Crespo, and Elizabeth Jenkins.

I am in utter gratitude to Marci Shimoff and Terri Cole for their kind and generous endorsements.

I'm so grateful for all the support, encouragement, and wise suggestions from all my dear friends and family members—the pure angels who are my parents, Christian and Martine Marlier, and my sister, Laetitia Marlier, as well as Eran Westwood, Tina Cullum, Adriane Boff, Justine Ma, Ramin Bahrani, Colleen De Bellefonds, Kim Snyder, Sara Wright, Kate Doyle and many more.

To my fabulous illustrator, Leo Schiavina, I say thanks and more thanks for bringing his talent and creativity to the project and helping bring my vision to life. Some of my most fun and rewarding moments of this whole process came from working with him!

I want to thank my (now friend) and agent during the Publishizer crowdfunding campaign, Julia Guirado, who brought to the process not only a wealth of skills, information, and support, but also a passion and commitment I never dreamed of.

I also gratefully acknowledge the hard work and enthusiasm of my wonderful and skilled editor and project manager from Belle Isle Books, Grace Ball. She's been so patient, wise, and kind, just as Christina Kann, my marketing expert, has—thank you!

I give thanks to each and every person who supported *Odette's Alphabet* in the crowdfunding campaign, giving me the clarity and confidence that I needed to keep going, embracing the wonderful unknown.

I am grateful to my family, who has and continues to influence the person I am and celebrate what I do.

And I bow to one of the most sacred relationships of all, the one with my daughter, Emma. Just as I shape who she is, she shapes who I am. She teaches me the importance of connection and understanding, patience, persistence, and forgiveness. She brings meaning and joy to my life. Through the great many opportunities and challenges of being her maman, I am constantly reminded that teaching meditation and mindfulness are about seeing the sacred in the mundane and living as if all of life is sacred, because it truly is.

I also want to acknowledge you, the reader, parent, caretaker, teacher; and you, powerful and wonderful children, for taking the time to read or listen to Odette and practice the activities that I invite you to make yours. Let this be a gentle guide and companion. I trust that it will make space for great connections, both with yourself—maybe becoming your own best friend—as well as with others.

And above all: have fun!

Love,

Sandrine

About the Author

SANDRINE MARLIER woke up one day in her New York apartment feeling out of sorts. She realized that no matter how many trips around the world her modeling career would take her on, it was only a journey within that would bring her peace. Eventually she trained with world-renowned meditation teacher davidji. It led to the inspiration for this book: she found herself drawing an ant and a sound: A, the beginning of all beginnings.

Sandrine is a mother, meditation teacher, transformational coach, and Reiki practitioner. She shares free meditations on Instagram (@sandrinemarlier) about healing and empowerment. You can connect with her through her website: www.sandrinemarlier.com

About the Illustrator

LEONARDO SCHIAVINA was born and raised in Italy. He moved to Barcelona, Spain, in 2014, where he obtained his master's degree. While there, Leo worked for many studios and agencies before founding his own graphic collective, Collettivo Mare, in 2015. He's been working as an art director and graphic designer for branding, illustration, and editorial design projects worldwide, from Spain to Israel to the US.

Leo is passionate about aesthetic graphic design and illustration, as well as music and photography, and he loves mixing them in a unique and genuine style.

Finally, Leo is a restless nomad, who loves living in different countries and cities. He's currently based in Tenerife, Canary Islands.

Printed in the USA
CPSIA information can be obtained
at www.ICGtesting.com
LVHW061236211123
764519LV00023BA/740